Spaceports & Spidersilk

February 2024

Edited by
Marcie Lynn Tentchoff

Spaceports & Spidersilk
February 2024
Edited by Marcie Lynn Tentchoff

Story and art copyrights owned by the respective authors and artists
Cover art "Moustronaut" by Ann Hoekstra
Cover design by Laura Givens

First Printing, February 2024

Hiraeth Publishing
P.O. Box 1248
Tularosa, NM 88352
www.hiraethsffh.com
e-mail: hiraethsubs@yahoo.com

From the Editor

What does the future hold? I think everyone wonders. On each final day of December people gather to eat, drink, listen to music, and watch the last minutes of the old year tick away while trying to decide what they want, hope, and even pledge for the next.

The future is complicated. Some things can be easily predicted. Schooling will almost certainly continue to exist in the future. Subjects will be taught. Students will sit at desks or tables, and scribble notes (both on the subject being taught, and to each other) while teachers hand out information along with assignments. But will they scribble those notes on paper? Even now electronics of various types are becoming common in classrooms. Will the desks students sit at be halfway across the world from the instructors who teach them? Or across multiple worlds? Will the subjects being taught remain the same, or will the middle schoolers of the future be learning how to build things that will save people from other planets? Will they even be directly apprenticing for difficult jobs aboard different space craft?

And what about the more social aspects of the future? Will the people we care about still be near to us, or will they be off on new adventures, leaving us behind?

Stories. Poems. Various futures, and worlds, and events. In the end, while we can imagine many possibilities, our only personal choice is to try to decide how we might face them. Will we be strong enough to stay true to ourselves, and to our friends? Will we be able to help people, even if it puts us at risk? Will we, when all is said and done, be open to the new encounters the future will bring?

Welcome to the February issue of Spaceports & Spidersilk. Read. Imagine. And try to be ready for what comes next!

Mellie

The Adventures of a Teenage Vampire

Meet Mellie, an adolescent vampire, as she travels to Italy and New York to discover roots, make friends, and of course get into trouble. Fun adventures for the whole family.

https://www.hiraethsffh.com/product-page/mellie-the-adventures-of-a-teenage-vampire-by-debby-feo

Pyra and the
Tektites
Aquarium in Space

Pyra, age thirteen, is running away from home in the Asteroid Belt because she's not doing well in school. Her parents want to send her to Mars for school, and she doesn't want to go. She sneaks aboard a cargo shuttle, and falls asleep in the hold. When she awakens, she finds herself in free-fall; the shuttle has been seized by the Tektites, a group of rebel pirates . . .

. . . and the adventures begin!

Order a copy of this thrilling adventure here:

https://www.hiraethsffh.com/product-page/pyra-and-the-tektites-1-by-tyree-campbell

Adopted Child

By Teri Santitoro

Imp, now 13, has awakened from stasis by MA, the ship's computer, to find that everyone else has been killed by a highly infectious disease. She is alone on the ship. But she is about to have visitors.

The *Greentown,* a salvage ship, has spotted a derelict and is about to board her for salvage rights. The crew is blissfully unaware of what happened to the people on the derelict. Soon enough they will find out...but will it be too late? And what of the girl who now controls the derelict?

To everyone involved, everything is new... and potentially lethal.

Ordering Link:

https://www.hiraethsffh.com/product-page/adopted-child-by-t-santitoro

The Adventures of Colo Collins & Tama Toledo in Space and Time
By Tyree Campbell

Out on their first date, high school seniors Colo Collins and Tama Toledo are invited aboard a spaceship and offered the chance to intervene in various events in the Universe. These events can range from stopping an asteroid from striking a planet to helping someone find her house keys. But there's a catch: both Colo and Tama have to agree that an intervention should be performed . . . and sometimes they'll have to perform the intervention themselves!

Ordering Link:

https://www.hiraethsffh.com/product-page/adventures-of-colo-collins-tama-toledo-in-space-and-time-by-tyree-campbell

Luke and Odett
James Fitzsimmons

Glancing at the alien girl out the corner of his eye, Luke Castellano barked a command at his robot: "Hobbs, go home!"

The six-inch tall mechanism with wiry antennae, spindly arms, and treadmill feet stopped roaming about the rocket's cabin, rolled to an electrical socket, and plugged itself in. Luke smiled with pride even though his most recent middle school creation was but a modified vacuum cleaner.

"Hobbs finds his own way by radio signal to a charging port, Odett."

Odett Elb of Canto smirked and said, "Cute, if you want to sweep up."

Odett went back to work on a scholarly paper she'd tried to talk Luke through that used math he couldn't fathom. Luke knew that middle school on Canto was academically beyond his middle school on Earth, but could Odett's classmates create anything like Hobbs?

"Well," Luke said, "Hobbs can protect itself with an electric charge."

Odett looked up sharply, sweeping away curls of orange hair from lavender skin. "Oh?"

Luke unplugged Hobbs from the socket and brought it to Odett. "Go ahead, Odett, touch him, anywhere."

Odett tentatively felt the top of the robot's head near the antennae.

"Hobbs, defend!" Luke said.

Odett snapped her hand back and shook it. "A stiff shock. Impressive."

"My dad doesn't approve," Luke said with a toss of his head. "Also, I'm the only one who can power the bot up and down. I use my thumbprint." He pressed his thumb into a well on the neck of the robot. The robot's arms drooped, and its lights went out.

"Mmm," Odett said, "the bots we design in class have many more functions." She went back to work.

Luke observed Odett's ears—similar to a human's but with even more rivulets and channels. He knew Cantonians could hear high frequencies, like a dog, and was curious to know more. "What's it like, Odett, hearing high pitched sounds?"

Odett shrugged. "It's okay, like background hum. I can make out Hobbs' hum blended with other equipment on board the ship."

"The hum doesn't bother you?"

"Only when a pattern stands out. That's annoying."

The rocket lurched as they exited the wormhole that provided a shortcut from Earth to Canto. Luke's and Odett's parents were collaborating on a project to develop quantum thread for exploring black holes, and the two families would travel between the two planets as work progressed. It was now the Castellano's turn to spend a few months on Canto with the Elbs. The planet lay dead ahead, and Luke shivered at the thought of attending a semester of middle school there. But he also looked forward to telling his classmates on Earth stories of space and adventure.

Luke smirked as he watched Odett work. Her English was excellent, but he couldn't tell if she addressed him in a snooty way on purpose, or if it was just her alien manner. He was having a rough time picking up Cantonian tongue, and the grown-up tone she used with him wasn't helping. He took Hobbs across the cabin to his study area, out of Odett's sight. With his thumb he powered the robot down, then up, then down, then up, then down, then up, then down.

Odett called out, "Okay, Luke, that's enough!"

Suddenly, something crashed into the hull, and the rocket shuddered.

Over a speaker came the voice of Luke's mom: "We've been hit by debris! Prepare to land!"

Luke and Odett buckled into their seats. The rocket was jerking from side to side as Luke saw a planet come into view through a port hole. The planet was fiery red with volcanoes spewing lava and ash. The rocket righted itself and descended, coming to a soft landing.

"A neighboring planet," Odett said looking out the window. "I don't think anyone ever comes here."

Odett's dad entered their cabin. "Took a hit on the starboard side. We'll be okay while we make repairs. Probably a stabilizer got knocked loose."

The two middle schoolers and their parents looked out over the planet's horizon as the hatch opened and the gangplank lowered. Sulphur, carried by a warm wind, entered the ship.

"Luckily, we can access the stabilizer from a step just outside the hatch," Odett's dad said as he carefully stepped out onto the gangplank. He opened a panel on the ship's hull and pulled out a component. "Looks okay, just got jostled loose."

As he inspected the component, the rocket shook abruptly, and a computer chip fell out of the component, wind carrying the chip some meters to the planet's surface.

"We need that chip!" Odett's dad said.

Odett's mom shook her head. "This planet is volcanically and seismically active! It's full of huge arthropods—like crabs!"

"We can send Hobbs," Luke said. "Let me upload a picture of the chip to him."

Odett's dad carefully pulled out a similar chip from the stabilizer, which Luke photographed and uploaded to Hobbs. Then Luke sent the robot down the gangplank toward its target, and the group cheered when it vacuumed up the chip.

Then a monstrous crab crawled out from a hole and reached for Hobbs.

"Hobbs, defend!" Luke yelled from the hatch.

The crab touched the robot then jerked its claw and backed away.

"Hobbs, go home!" Luke commanded, but before the robot could get away, five more crabs crawled out of the ground.

"The crabs must think Hobbs is an intruder," Luke's mom said, "with his thin arms and antennae."

The crabs backed Hobbs against a rock wall, and Hobbs disappeared into a hole.

"The robot went down a lava tube," Odett's mom said.

Luke's dad retrieved a blaster from the cabin, ran down the gangplank, and shooed away the crabs from the lava wall. When the crew joined him, Odett and her parents listened closely.

"He's trying to find his way out," Odett's dad said. "We can hear him rolling around. But the tunnel's too small for us to fit."

"I can go in," Odett said. "I can fit."

"Me too!" Luke added. "Hobbs only obeys me."

Odett's and Luke's parents looked at each other.

"We need that chip," Luke's dad said. "We can send them in tethered, with flashlights and a radio."

His dad ran to the ship, and when he returned dragging a length of cord, they all looked to the sky as a huge insect swooped down at them with a deafening buzz. Its wings beat so fast, ash from the surface flew in their faces.

"A giant bumblebee?" Luke's dad said, aiming his blaster and firing a slit into the attacker's abdomen. He jumped back as green ooze splashed on the ground, the giant bee crashing nearby. "Let's work fast," he said.

After he tied Luke and Odett together at their waists and the opposite end of the tether to the ship, the pair squatted and slithered into the tunnel, Odett leading the way. The parents returned quickly to the ship.

The lava tube was cool and breathable, but the path was tight, enveloping them in darkness.

"Hobbs isn't too far off," Odett said.

Luke felt his pulse race, his initial excitement now giving way to dread. In one very close spot, their bodies crushed against each other while Odett paused to get a bearing on Hobbs' hum. Luke feared Odett would detect his heart pumping wildly. He felt the palm of her hand rest on the back of his, which relaxed him.

"This way," she said, taking a fork to the right. "We're getting close!"

They stopped at the edge of a deep pit, their flashlights finding Hobbs at the bottom, running around in circles.

"He's stuck!" Luke said. "Help me down."

They untied themselves, and Luke climbed down into the pit as Odett held the tether. He powered off the robot with his thumb. "Better save whatever energy he has left."

He opened the vacuum compartment, took out the chip, and gave Odett a thumbs-up. He radioed the ship: "Got it!"

Luke tied the tether around Hobbs, and Odett pulled the robot up. Then Luke climbed out. The two nodded to each other and set off on their return, following the tether.

As they moved along the tube through twists and turns, they came upon intense heat. The way was suddenly blocked by steaming, hot red lava. With the tether trapped under searing liquid, Luke gave the cord a yank, and it snapped in two.

"Mom, dad, the tunnel is blocked by lava!" Luke radioed.

"Lord!" his dad radioed back. "There are many openings in the lava wall outside the ship. Find another way!"

Luke turned to Odett. "Can you detect the hum of the ship from here?"

Odett shook her head. "Too far away. But what about—"

Luke had been carrying Hobbs and guessed at her idea. He set the robot down and powered it up. "Hopefully, he has some energy left. Hobbs, go home!"

The little machine reversed course, taking them down one fork and then another, going left, then going right. Luke and Odett had to bend, twist, and scurry to keep up. Finally they saw daylight, and exited an opening in the lava wall only meters from the one they'd entered. They hurried up the ship's gangplank and gave Odett's dad the missing chip. In minutes, with the chip inserted into the stabilizer and the gangplank raised, the rocket blasted off just as lava spewed from several tubes, flooding the area in molten rock.

###

Once under way, Hobbs was recharging, Luke was lounging in his seat, and Odett was working on her paper. Luke could make out Canto rapidly approaching, and he took a deep breath. The adventure in the lava tube had momentarily let him forget about Canto middle school, but now reality was setting in on him again.

He started when Odett said, "Hobbs is a wonderful bot."

He nodded. "Hobbs might have found his way out of the tunnel if he hadn't fallen into that pit. Maybe I can fix that with sensors and a headlamp."

Odett moved across the cabin to him. "You'll do fine on Canto." She looked around the cabin then kissed him on the cheek. "I'll help you."

Luke smiled as a warm glow spread over him, and he suddenly looked forward to Canto.

Amaruq's Island

Lisa Lahey

In the iciest ocean floats Amaruq's Island
Where Arctic Bay water sparkles with
    diamonds
Nestled in mountains wondrously bold
Lies breathtaking beauty and legends of old

Here in the island lives young Amaruq
Whose name boasts her totem, the mighty
    gray wolf
Amaruq is young, her spirit is strong
Her black hair is braided, her eyes slanted
    and long

Inside Amaruq's house, plain and humble
A husky who barks, a baby who tumbles
Amaruq cooks with her mother Inuit dishes
She knits winter sweaters with colorful fishes

In the spring when its warm Amaruq gathers
    crowberries
And cloudberry and vetch and wild ground
    cherries
She bakes them in pies and magical cakes
The berries grant wishes that Amaruq makes

Aput her grandmother, loving and kind
Weaves Amaruq's head with legends
    entwined
Of spirits and dieties and magical creatures

Like Sedna the mermaid and Orca who
    breaches

In Amaruq's dreams she flies above snow
She floats in the daylight and sees down
below
Families of otter and elusive narwhals
The woods where she hunts spotted
    nightjars

In darkness Amaruq sails on a glacier of ice
Through the icy ocean toward northern lights
She soars into the skies and down through
    the gale
Riding a fin of the great Bowhead whale

In the iciest ocean floats Amaruq's Island
Where Arctic Bay water sparkles with
    diamonds
Nestled in mountains that are wondrously
    bold
Lies breathtaking beauty and legends of old

Slip-Stitch
Megan Archibeque

Nora enjoyed the walk best in the blue hour. The quiet that licked at the trees and put the animals to bed. Things felt at peace, and there was no quiet back home.

Avi told her of the dangers often.

The night-time forest will eat you alive," she would whisper. "It'll spit you out bones and Tally will cry."

"And you?"

Avi would tilt her chin toward the sky.

"I will let what's left of you turn yellow in the sun."

Nora only went into the forest as the sun set from then on. If the forest ate her up Avi would starve and she knew that well.

The trees leaned in to greet her as she walked into their shadows. Whispered to her of the mellow things that had happened in the daylight.

In her hands she held only a pair of kitchen scissors. In her pocket a teaspoon of sugar to keep away the worst of the nasties.

"Yellow for joy. Yellow for protection," she kneeled to snip a mushroom from the earth. Smiling as what was left grew over with baby yellows, a whole new patch by the full moon. One would do. She tucked the first mushroom into her pocket. She would need it tonight; never before had she gone past the

Slip-Stitch Tree and though she would not say it out loud, the stories of what lay beyond made her heart pound.

The path Nora had stomped down over the many moon cycles had disappeared with the recent storm. She would use her last bit of candle if she must.

Tonight she would walk far, and to places entirely unknown. The boy-no-longer who had made this journey before, the only one who ever had in their village, had told her how to get over. He had been tossed back with shaking hands and eyes never quite seeing what was right in front of him.

"I've seen all there is." He would say. He would press his hands against Nora's cheeks and tell her she was one thousand times braver than he, she was meant to journey beyond.

She had chosen tonight for her age. Exactly half-way to The Going Year. It felt like the time to ruin her sanity if she was meant to. Though from bravery, or foolishness, she was certain this would not be her fate.

An Eye opened before her, glowing dull green and judging the human-ness of her. Nora took three steps back, and gave the Eye her best curtsy. It stared at her for a few more aching seconds, time always seemed to stretch as these night-things considered you.

The Eye blinked closed. Most likely gone. Nora continued.

"Green, green, green," she whispered, as a rush of wind blew through the thin trees. A rain of leaves fell to the ground. Soon would come the Harvest Moon, and the trees shook off their summer skins as they felt the hum of such a special time drawing near. Nora stuck a leaf in her pocket.

These hours alone were her favorite thing. She had spent two whole summers sleeping out here all the nights except the full ones. Making beds in hollowed-out trees or in the high grasses. Avi had never dared come after her. Only once the sun was peeking from behind the mountains would she run into the trees to drag Nora home.

But Nora had not slept here since the night The Screeching had found her dreaming. She had never told Avi nor Tally what had happened.

Avi had found her in their bed the next night, staring at the ceiling with eyes so deeply worried the eldest sister had not wanted to know. And she'd found her there every morning since, even if Nora did not return until near morning.

The Granny Tree was bursting with apples this time of year. The tree more apple than branch. Nora only had to flick the lowest hanging fruit for it to fall to the still damp soil at the creeping feet of the tree. The tree watched her do it and said nothing.

Nora liked this, The Granny approving of Nora as a taker of their treasure. A good sign for what was to come.

The apple hit the ground in six pieces and quickly reduced itself to dirt again leaving behind the seeds. Nora picked them up one by one. Placing them in her pocket with the leaf and the candle and the mushroom and the sugar. She moved on. Visions of Avi's apple pie, made with these apples when you still had to yank, made her stomach rumble. They'd eaten that pie for breakfast, dinner, midnight meal until Tavvy had gotten ill.

She'd been really cruel about it. Apples thrown and little-boy feelings hurt deeply.

Most days of Nora's were head-full. Thoughts so shoved on top of one another they'd leak from her eyes and punch harder than she meant to. But in the deep, dark of the wood a whisper was a rarity. She had no need for fists here.

A twig breaking in half echoed around her. Nora turned. No one, but the attention of the trees worried her, all of them leaning into where she stood small and almost unafraid in the dark. What did they know she did not?

Another twig. A leaf fell, tapping her shoulder. Nora jumped. There was someone around.

"Hello?" She spoke, breaking her months of only whispers here and there.

The nothing that answered made her feel silly. *Do not be a scaredy cat.*

Nora continued her path, pulling out the kitchen scissors in case. Her thoughts wandered as they often did to The Screeching, always returning to a long, sharp fingernail drawing a line of blood up her arm. When she'd dreamt that night it had been all red, dripping from the sky and getting in her eyes, it had stung. She was grateful for the shove. Had she woken only a moment later it would have been too late. *It'll spit you out bones and Tally will cry.*

Another twig.

When Nora turned this time she saw a girl.

She was so stark-white Nora thought she was glowing. Like the moon.

"You shouldn't be out here," Nora said.

The girl stared with huge dark eyes. Still as a statue. Nora did not know her from town; she thought and thought as they stared at each other.

"Go away." Nora said.

The girl's dress swung lazily around her knees. The fabric had holes in it and in the holes were shoved leaves. A few fell to the forest floor.

Nora held up her scissors. "I mean it. Get out of my forest."

The girl smiled with pale lips and shook her head.

"Are you going to hurt me?" Nora asked.

The girl was still for a long time before she shook her head again. The smile on her lips did not feel quite kind.

They stood looking at each other, the hand that held the scissors did not lower.

"I'm on a quest." Nora broke away, her heart deep in the pit of her stomach. "Don't follow me."

She walked then, walked and walked for a while or at least a few minutes without looking back.

The idea that she was once again alone seemed too good to be true. She could see the roots of the Slip-Stitch Tree beginning their maze along the ground; not much farther to go.

Another twig broke.

Nora swung to face the girl not two feet away, the broken twig held in her hands.

The curiosity barely overcame the fear. "I thought you were stepping on them."

The girl dropped the pieces to the ground.

"Tell me what you're up to?" Nora held the scissors to the girl's long neck. "And maybe I'll tell you."

The girl tilted her head from side to side.

Nora huffed a heavy sigh and turned away from the creeper girl, dancing carefully along the roots now thick as tree logs. She had to be careful to balance, when she stole a glance back the girl's toes hovered inches above in the air.

Nora shivered.

The forest once again was silent and content in its watching.

The Slip-Stitch Tree loomed high and mighty before them. It towered, watching like a God of the woods from its place at its center, a thousand limbs stretching, a thousand roots reaching. The first tree planted after The Scratch thousands of years ago.

"This is important." Nora whispered to the girl now floating beside her, gawking at the tree with wide black eyes.

She took the yellow mushroom from her pocket and ate it, cap and stem.

Beyond The Slip-Stitch was utter darkness. The Tree stood guard to something unknown to all. Something even Nora had never found the courage to journey within.

Darkness that swallowed and breathed, and was held back only by the great Slip-Stitch.

That was where The Screeching and all its friends came from.

Standing on just the roots had made Nora's ears begin to ring. She looked at the girl who was looking back expectantly, and took steps farther than she'd ever gone before.

Eyes opened against the trunk of the tree. Nora stopped but the girl floated on. The eyes blinked and stared but made no move to stop her.

Nora watched the girl float and wondered if she came from that place, the more she looked at her and the leaves slipping from her dress, the length of her thin unused legs, the less girl and more creature she became.

The girl reached the black. The Eyes or the tree or the whole forest itself was humming a dull, continuous note. Nora's nose was running and her feet felt hot. She ran forward in a careful zigzag along the roots as they twisted around each other, becoming a mound at the base of the tree. When she looked up the Eyes were focused on her, when she got as close as she could she curtsied at them.

The girl shook her head at Nora as if to say, "do not be afraid." She reached out her long thin fingers toward the beyond, and through it, up until her elbow was invisible. The darkness swirled around her, tendrils reaching up her forearms.

Nora gasped. But the girl left her arm there, head tilted in wait.

"What are you doing?" Nora whispered, barely able to hear herself over the hum.

The girl smiled then and retracted her arm from the thick fog, it let her go.

Nora did not understand.

Ladybugs.

At least a hundred ladybugs danced along the girl's arm. She cupped her hands and immediately the ladybugs filled her palms. They buzzed around her and made themselves comfortable against her ghostly skin. The girl tilted her head back, her mouth open as if to laugh.

They did not touch Nora.

The plan had vanished from her thoughts. She thought desperately, reaching at bits of things as the pounding in her head got angrier. She was not yet welcome here.

"Ask permission," Nora said. Remembering the boy who was not a boy anymore, who had made this journey once and returned in time to turn fifteen with nothing changed on the outside save for always-shaking hands.

The girl as white as the moon was stone-still again and Nora wondered if she was waiting for her.

"I seek an audience!" She yelled up at the Eyes and The Slip-Stitch Tree.

The hum grew louder, and the tree—the whole tree leaned forward, creaking loud enough to wake the village miles away.

The Eyes were a deep dark shade of nighttime. They did not blink, and Nora knew the tree was seeing her through them. Seeing not only the skin, and the hair, and the kitchen scissors. It was sifting through the grains of sugar at the bottom of her pocket. It was flipping through her memories like a picture book.

What would you like, careful walker of my woods?

Nora shuddered as the ancient voice crawled through her whole body, wrapping itself around her bones and rushing through her blood.

"I want to know," she said. Stealing a glance at the girl with the deep dark eyes, a smile on her lips, the ladybugs dancing around her. "I want to fly."

The Slip-Stitch creaked and groaned, it filled Nora's head with something like laughter.

Go on then.

Nora thought for a moment the solid roots had disappeared from below her feet. When she looked down she was hovering above them just like the girl.

The girl reached out her hands and the ladybugs began to circle Nora, she laughed and let them find their way into her hair and kiss her skin.

"Do we go?"

The girl nodded.

Nora looked back to the still woods holding their breath in wait for her. A village home, a warm bed, an older sister, a little brother, a life she knew well all somewhere behind them.

"Will you help me get back when it's time?"

The girl nodded again, pointing to Nora's pocket.

Nora pulled out two of the apple seeds.

"We'll make a Granny-Promise then."

The girl took the seed from Nora's open palm, where her fingers touched became pleasantly warm.

She placed the seed on her tongue. Nora did the same.

They chewed. Spit their seeds on the ground.

The girl held out her hand.

Nora took it.

"Will everything change now?"

The girl nodded.

Nora took a deep breath, her heart pounding as they turned toward the darkness.

She thought to herself, her last thoughts before everything, *I am not a scaredy cat. I am the bravest. A hero half-written. When I go I'll go in greatness.*

The ladybugs sang to go on, go on, and with the warm hand of the girl in hers, she flew beyond.

Crashing the Party
Grant Swenson

Adain stormed into his tiny, humid cabin and switched off the communication box next to the door. He knew his action broke the third rule of the interplanetary cargo ship Ophilla, but he didn't care. He wanted time alone.

Breathing deep, Adain listened to the cyclic hum of the power relays to calm his nerves. He had endured another frustrating day in the engine room. The chief engineer Tomas finished Adain's repair work once again because he thought Adain was too slow. Tomas rarely allowed Adain the time to prove himself a capable apprentice engineer.

Adain cringed at his dirty, sweaty, gaunt face reflected in the chipped mirror by the bed. Sick of the overwhelming heat and wondering if he would ever be cold again, he rubbed the grease off his cheeks and plopped down on the hard mattress. After six months on the job, twelve-year-old Adain wished for a shift free of criticism and Tomas' glare.

Crawling under his threadbare blanket, Adain drifted into a quiet slumber.

Awruga! Awruga! Awruga! Alarms blared and the ship banked hard to starboard. Adain thudded to the floor, scraped against the warm metal, and slammed into the wall.

His eyes adjusting slowly to the red flashing light, Adain winced at the sharp pain in his shoulder. Twelve years of childhood drills forced his body into action. He scurried into the darkness under the bed, expecting the rest of the crew to oversee the emergency. Thirty-six-year-old Tomas would surely fix the problem right away.

The lack of chatter on the net unnerved him, leading to the sudden realization that he turned off the communication box at the end of his shift. Adain's stomach turned when he imagined Tomas yelling at him for hours.

Adain crawled out from under the bed and stumbled across the room. He switched on the communication box and pressed the call button. "Tomas, this is Adain. What's happening? Over."

No response.

Adain punched the flat panel and hurried out of the bedroom.

His feet pounded against the metal grate floor, and he squeezed through the narrow hall, dodging row upon row of multi-colored pipes. He slid to a stop in front of the engine room and the worn, blue plastic door opened automatically.

Over the years, repairs and improvements had led to the engine growing into a jumble of pipes, wires, and gears extending in all directions. Tomas understood every twist and turn, but the complexity overwhelmed Adain.

"Tomas, I'm here if you need me," Adain yelled over the sputtering valves and shrieking gears.

No one answered.

Adain traversed the cables littering the floor and the warm pipes snaking away from the engine. He checked every nook and cranny without success.

Sweat pooling on his brow, he leaned against the engine core and struggled to breathe. He rejected the fleeting thought running through his head: I'm all alone. He had never felt truly alone growing up or training for this apprenticeship.

Adain's head pounded in rhythm to the alarms. The control room on the other side of the ship had the only button to shut off the alarm.

Adain barreled out of the engine room and climbed the ladder to the catwalk running along the cargo bay. He slid through an oval door and froze. The cargo bay was empty. The crates filling the space only a day before were gone. Adain's legs shook and he grasped the railing for support.

The ship rumbled and roared. Adain's heart raced. He stared straight ahead, forced his legs into a jog, and charged across the catwalk. Adain stepped into the control room and fell to his knees. Not a single crew member remained. He wanted to rescind his wish of a day all to himself. This wasn't what he meant.

He dragged himself to the center of the room and slumped into the big, green, cushiony captain's chair. He turned off the alarm and stared at Saturn's largest moon, Titan, filling the view-screen.

His ears adjusted slowly to the lack of an alarm, but he continued to hear a muted whine from a human source. Adain isolated it to the space by the pilot's console and trudged over to investigate. The ship's pilot Harel was curled up in a ball on the metal floor. Harel was only six months older than Adain, but she had already achieved full crew member status.

"It's my fault," Harel said. "It's my fault."

"Am I glad to see you," Adain said as he pulled her from the floor. "I thought I was all alone."

Harel reacted gradually, flattening her wrinkled orange and yellow striped shirt. She cleared away a long strand of blonde hair, exposing her silver eyes. She wiped away her tears. "Do I know you?"

"My name is Adain. We met when I joined the crew."

Harel squinted. "Oh, right. I think I remember. It's been a long time."

"Are you okay?"

Harel shuddered. "I think so. Please ignore what you saw. Remind me again what you do?"

"I'm Tomas' apprentice."

"An engineer." Harel slid into her chair. "Good. I need your help. The engine is only running at forty percent efficiency and three maneuvering thrusters aren't responding. If we don't fix everything, we'll drop into Titan's atmosphere and crash."

"What happened?" Adain asked. "I woke to the alarm and freaked out a little when I noticed the crew and cargo were gone."

"How long were you sleeping?" Harel tapped her console to display the log. "A tug arrived to take the cargo to the surface. The crew went with them to celebrate the captain's birthday. I stayed behind to watch the ship. I guess Tomas left you behind, too. What did you do to get on his bad side?"

"Everything. But that doesn't explain the alarm."

"We hit something. Or something hit us. Either way, I wasn't paying attention. It damaged the engine and the three thrusters. It also knocked us from our safe orbit. I didn't expect to survive because Tomas was down on the planet. I'm an exceptional pilot, but not a good engineer."

Adain gripped the console and his fingers slowly drained of color. "When I signed up for this job, I thought a cargo vessel was the safest and easiest choice."

"This wasn't the plan." Before Adain said another word, Harel added, "I don't need to hear you complain. I need you to fix the engine."

"Can we talk this over?"

Harel glared at Adain. "The first rule of Ophilla is to listen to your superior. I have superiority. That means what I say goes. Fix the engines, now."

Adain stared at Harel and knew she wouldn't waver based on her unflinching gaze. "Fine. But I can't fix it fast. It will take me a week to figure out what the problem is. It may take even longer to fix it."

"We don't have a week."

The ship rolled suddenly and knocked Adain off his feet. The alarm resounded. Adain pulled himself to the engineer's console. The planetary shields strained under the pressure from Titan's atmosphere.

"We're stuck in an orbit that leads to disaster," Harel said. "If you don't fix the engines in less than an hour, the planet's atmosphere will crush us."

"What about the alternative?"

"What alternative?"

Adain displayed the sensor readouts. "We land on Titan. The aero-jets aren't showing any faults. When were they last evaluated?" Harel shrugged. "Plus, the crew is already down there. It will be perfect."

Harel shook her head. "I don't do planetary or moon landings."

"You can't or you won't?"

"Both. I've never had to perform one."

"I thought you couldn't be a certified pilot until you landed on a planet or a moon."

"If you're an expert like I am, you only need to pass the written exam."

"Well, here's your chance at the real thing. I know I can fix the shields in less than an hour. The aero-jets will get us the rest of the way. Either you land on Titan, or we burn up on entry. The choice is yours."

Harel shifted in place and scrutinized their trajectory. "I still don't like it, but I don't want to die today." She turned off the alarm.

"Good choice." Adain hurried to the back of the control room, ripped off the access panel, and slid down the ladder.

The planetary shield generator banged and clunked. The gears slipped. The stench of burnt plastic and rotting oil oozed from the walls.

Adain punched the call button on the communication box. "Harel, how may minutes do we have?"

"Fifty minutes top," Harel replied.

The odor reminded Adain of a basic repair he completed in his first week on the ship. A deep dive across the rings of Saturn fried the power converters. He examined the line of green boxes connected to a series of red pipes. Ten of the fourteen boxes were charred to a crisp.

Replacing each one took longer than Adain expected. Sweat drenched his blue shirt by the time he finished.

He pressed the call button. "That should have fixed the problem."

The communication line crackled. "The shield power is still dropping. We only have ten minutes left."

Adain scratched his head. The power converter replacement worked the last time. He turned his attention to the main body of the generator. The slipping gears connected only half of the time. He needed to tighten the central rotor to re-align the system.

Yanking a wrench from the wall, he slipped it over the locking nut and realized the entire connection was stuck shut. Tomas had delayed major repairs even longer than Adain thought. They never landed on a planet or moon, so why care about the shield generator? What did that mean for the aero-jets?

Adain struggled to move the locking nut. His body tensed. His arms shook. His injured shoulder throbbed.

Nothing moved.

Harel called over the communication line. "Less than five minutes."

Drawing in a deep breath, Adain wedged his body between the ceiling and the wrench and pushed with every muscle in his body.

The ship rattled and shook. The alarm blared. The outer hull brushed Titan's atmosphere.

Adain twisted in place and pushed harder.

The walls glowed and the hull creaked, moments away from ripping apart.

Adain screamed.

The wrench moved.

The nut turned.

The rotor shifted.

The gears locked.

Power flowed through the new converters.

Adain collapsed to the floor and cradled his injured shoulder.

The communication line hummed. "Shields at ninety percent."

The ship dove into Titan's atmosphere, and the shields held.

Adain dragged himself up the ladder to the control room and over to the green captain's chair. "Bring us down safe, Harel."

With the hull groaning, the cargo ship Ophilla screamed through Titan's atmosphere.

"That's the plan," Harel said with a tense smirk. "Go make sure the aero-jets work."

Adain raced out of the control room, along the catwalk, and down to the engine room. Checking the system read-outs from each of the four jets, he positioned himself next to the aft engine on the port side thinking it was the most likely to fail. Once they dropped far enough into the atmosphere, he started the jet initiation sequence for each one. The jet he worried the most about roared to life without issue, but the jet on the port side sputtered and shut down.

He threw open the panel leading to the injection system and unbolted the thermal barrier. Evaluating the nozzle, he noticed it was clogged. Grabbing an awl from the workbench, he dug into the goo and pried it off. He assessed the injector one more time, bolted down the thermal barrier, and slammed the panel closed. He restarted the initiation sequence, and the jet belched into operation.

Adain hurried back to the control room and jumped into the captain's chair. He stared at the rapidly approaching surface in the view screen. A sparkling blue and purple ocean embraced a series of ragged mountain ranges. The water mesmerized him. He grew up on a mining colony in the asteroid belt and never spent time near large expanses of water.

"Find me somewhere to land!" Harel ordered.

Adain didn't acknowledge the request.

"Snap out of it, Adain," Harel shouted.

Adain's gaze didn't waver. "What?"

"Find me somewhere to land, now!"

Adain moved sluggishly. The control panel next to the captain's chair was a blur of dials and colors. He loosened his grip on the chair and blinked to refocus. He punched up the sensor array display. He didn't remember what all the symbols meant, but he knew the glowing yellow ball behind a nearby peak signaled life.

"There's a valley with a city on the port side beyond the mountain peak," Adain reported.

"That's no mountain. That's an iceberg," Harel said. "I hope your aero-jets get us there."

The ship banked hard to port and continued to descend steeply. The jets struggled to maintain enough altitude to clear the iceberg.

"We're not going to make it," Harel said.

The ship plunged toward the iceberg, every second dipping further below the peak.

Harel leaned away from her console. "Do something!"

Adain examined the safety controls. Tomas warned him repeatedly not to violate Ophilla's second rule about safety limits, but now wasn't the time to play it safe. Adain switched off the limits. "Fire the jets at full."

"They'll tear apart."

"We don't have a choice."

Harel drove the jets to maximum power.

The ship shook.

The jets sputtered.

The engine reverberated.

The ship rose gradually, but not enough to clear the peak.

"We're too heavy," Harel said.

The cargo bay was already empty. The water and fuel reserves were the only extra weight. Adain yanked at the dusty cover over the emergency release button, but it didn't budge.

The glorious purple iceberg filled the view screen. The ship was only moments away from a head-on collision.

Adain slipped his thin fingers around the edge of the cover and pried it loose. He pressed the button and held his breath. In the ship's belly, the bay doors creaked open, dropping the load of fuel and water.

The ship crept up slowly.

Adain braced for impact.

The ship scraped the iceberg peak and shattered ice in all directions. A high-pitch squeal echoed through the hull.

Sighing with relief, Adain collapsed into the captain's chair. "We made it."

After a quick discussion with the local authorities, Harel landed gracefully on an empty landing platform.

Their legs shaking, Adain and Harel walked through the empty ship. Each step rang hollow in the cavernous cargo bay. Adain opened the airlock and a cool, sweet breeze swept past him. Goosebumps raised on his arms.

The rest of the crew stood on the platform with the captain in front and Tomas behind him. The captain said, "Explain yourself."

"It was an emergency, sir," Harel said. "Something hit us and damaged the engine. Our only choice was landing on Titan. Without Adain's engineering support to fix the planetary shields and the aero-jets, we wouldn't be standing here, and the ship would be rubble."

"Happy birthday, sir," Adain said when the captain glanced his way.

"Thank you," the captain said. "Tomas, it's a good thing we picked up a new apprentice for you. Let me know when the ship is ready for our next mission."

"Yes, sir," Tomas said.

"Let's finish celebrating my birthday," the captain said.

Everyone except Tomas and Adain returned to the party raging at the landing facility.

"The repairs will be extensive," Tomas said, his gaze swapping between Adain and the ship. "Are you prepared for a grueling work schedule to fix everything?"

"Absolutely," Adain said.

"Good to hear," Tomas said. "Tomorrow we'll examine every inch of the ship. By the time we're done, you'll be able to handle any engineering job."

"Thank you, sir."

"I should be thanking you for saving the ship. That alone deserves a celebration. Let's join the party."

Dawn, on Dorva
Lisa Timpf

getting up before sunrise
Evie sneaks from the dome—
As the blue dwarf sun rises,
she jogs with bounding strides
through lilac mist.

Poetry Reviewed

Lauren McBride's *Aliens, Magic, and Monsters: A Speculative Collection (Science Fiction, Fantasy, and Horror)*, Hiraeth Publishing, September, 2023.

I read a lot of poetry collections. Some are sent to me by writer friends, some I have access to through various writing organizations and publications, and some I simply hear about and want to read.

The collection I'm reviewing today, *Aliens, Magic, and Monsters* by Lauren McBride, can easily fit into any of the above categories. I've read many of the poet's works before, and she is a regular contributor to Spaceports & Spidersilk. There's a reason for that. Her poems, especially the ones in this collection, are written such that they can be enjoyed and even loved by readers of all ages. Some are full of fun and humor, some are thoughtful, and some lean towards darker things, but all engage emotions and leave the reader feeling different and changed, even if that change takes the form of a sharp gasp at a nicely turned phrase or an all out laugh at an unexpected (and often diabolical) plot twist.

And all of the poems are accessible. Instead of (as far too many modern poets do) trying to put poetry on a pedestal and let all who wish to view it know that it is for only *special* people, McBride's poems do not attempt to gatekeep, but reach right into the hearts of readers, communicating thoughts and feelings clearly and beautifully. They paint pictures. They tell stories. They make us think. And if the poetic forms (and there are many different forms used in this book) themselves might confuse readers, McBride takes communication a step further, naming the form of each poem at its end, and then explaining how that form works at the end of the collection. From acrostics to zip one-breaths, each poetry type is defined and made clear, maybe even to the point of inspiring readers to attempt similar pieces.

But while the forms used are important, so too is the content of the poems themselves. These are poems that take us, as readers, to other places. From the opening of the collection, we are led to explore outwards. "Come Embrace Space" tells us to:

Book

your out-of-this-world

experience and getaway

today

by calling

"Affordable Space Vacations."

And so we do, heading out towards different stars. There we find out that parents across the universe have problems asking directions, even to visit family, and that the alien creatures may have many similarities to us, as well as their own ways of dealing with problems. Of *course* certain aliens might have better ways of playing music than we do, and of *course* a planet of sentient spiders would have slightly different requirements in the way of storage. The poems show us new ideas in ways that simply make sense.

When McBride switches from worlds of space and science fiction to realms more comprised of fantasy, that relatability just continues, but often with a slightly darker edge. From the child begging for a dragon (and who hasn't wanted a pet dragon?) to the were-creature in the rhyming poem "Lycanthropy," which reads:

I dread the change, the monthly fright:

the rage inside, the need to bite,

there is a feeling that these worlds, while still ones we can understand, might not be as safe and tame as those we see in the night sky. There is still humor (the poem "Spoiler Alert" is hilarious), but the wit seems sharper and more dangerous.

Which leads us to the collection's final section, one dealing with horror. Each of us has, I think, our own idea of what horrifies us. None of the poems in this collection should be enough to give readers nightmares, but many may make a chill run down one's spine. They show readers things that *might* be lurking in the dark. For example, "By the Foot of the Bed" reads:

> I never hang a foot
>
> off the edge of the bed
>
> for fear of toothy ghouls
>
> and other things un-dead

The worlds visited in the horror section are still riviting, and worthy of exploration, but cautiously, with the need for a solid exit plan in place, as is illustrated in "For in that Sleep, What Nightmares . . ."

> and if you see a silent scream
>
> while I lie trapped within a dream,
>
> then wake me from this hell replayed.

That, in the end, is a great thing about poetry collections, and *Aliens, Magic, and Monsters* in specific. In its pages, McBride gives us both bright and shadowed glimpses of alien places, peoples, and experiences, in ways we can understand and (sometimes with a wicked shudder) enjoy. But each depiction, while detailed enough to draw us in and engage us, leaves us room to imagine our own takes on the adventure, and our own way of dealing with both the joys and the terrors.

That is, after all, what the best of reading is all about.

Awkward Meet and Greet
Lauren McBride

For one thing,
They have three
eyes up on stalks,
spines for hair,
and tentacles for teeth.

But sure -
get mad at me
for staring.

Aliens, Magic, and Monsters
By Lauren McBride

Fun to read. Fun to write. *Aliens, Magic, and Monsters* features poems set in the unlimited and imaginative realm of science fiction, fantasy, and horror. The poems were chosen to showcase over twenty poetic forms from acrostiku to zip, from strict rhyme to free verse, and much more in between. There are guidelines included on how to write each type of poem. Try a sci(na)ku. At only six words, it's sure to interest even the youngest readers.

Type: Juvenile and Young Adult Poetry Manual
Ordering links:
Print: https://www.hiraethsffh.com/product-page/aliens-magic-and-monsters-by-lauren-mcbride

ePub: https://www.hiraethsffh.com/product-page/aliens-magic-and-monsters-by-lauren-mcbride-2

PDF: https://www.hiraethsffh.com/product-page/aliens-magic-and-monsters-by-lauren-mcbride-1

Winged Dragon

Vonnie Winslow Crist

If
Brian Rosenberger

If leaves were feathers and
Feathers were leaves,
Trees would fly and
Birds would fall.

If seeds were teeth and
Teeth were seeds,
Gardens would bite and
Smiles would grow.

If sharks were dogs and
Dogs were sharks,
Walks would become swims and
Bites would be much worse than barks.

If cats were dragons and
Dragons were cats,
Hairballs become balls of fire and
Mice had best beware.

A Little Lavender Magic
Megan Mahoney

The spell was being stubborn again. Georgie blew a curl out of her face with a huff and began again. Arborvitae for unchanging friendship, cyclamen for good-bye, forget-me-nots for...

Georgie sniffed and blinked, and the potion let out a sad little burp of slate smoke. She smacked her hand down on the table, making the bottles and jars quaver and clink.

"This is horrible!" she announced, collapsing onto the bench. "My best friend is leaving me forever, and I can't even make her a going-away gift. I'm the worst witch ever!"

Her toad, Vincent, blinked at her from the bench. Georgie sighed.

"Let me wallow a little, Vinny. I'm thirteen. I'm allowed to wallow."

Vincent inflated his vocal sac and let out an impressive errrp. Being her familiar, he could talk. He was just choosing not to. Georgie found that particularly annoying, especially on today of all days.

A knock sounded on the door of Georgie's shed. Without waiting for Georgie's permission, her mom poked her head in, making the chimes above the door ring aggressively. Georgie had cast holly berries and rhododendron flowers into the resin for protection and warning of danger, and the windchimes took their job a little too seriously.

"I know, I know," Georgie grumbled, and the windchimes gave one last wary tinkle before resuming their watchful silence.

"The party's in half an hour, baby," Mom said cheerfully. "Do you want to make some centerpieces? I'm sure Nadine would love that."

"I need to finish her present!" A note of panic slipped into Georgie's voice. "It's not done yet!"

Mom frowned over Georgie's shoulder at the mess on her desk. "Do you want my help? I can—"

"No, it has to be from me. That's the whole point!"

Mom sighed. "Okay, but hurry. And you need to be properly dressed for the event. Hat and charms at the very least."

"Okay, okay," Georgie muttered, already flipping through her botany notebook. Watercolor paintings, colored pencil sketches, dried leaves and petals and rattling seed pods filled the pages of the book, with Georgie's signature scrawl filling the space around them. She must be missing something, some kind of balance, or binding ingredient that would hold everything together. Maybe this current mix had too much of her sorrow—she couldn't even finish without weeping.

As she worked, she could hear the sounds of people assembling in the garden outside. Since her family's major source of power came from botany, they had one of the largest and most beautiful gardens in town, so Mom had decided to host events here in a fit of entrepreneurial spirit. Georgie loved making the bouquets for brides and the centerpieces for quinceanera receptions, and she didn't mind helping set up tables and chairs. Normally, she'd be out there welcoming guests and sprinkling a little extra magic on the flowers to make them especially vibrant.

But today she had to finish her gift.

"Let's try this," Georgie muttered. Arborvitae, basil for good wishes, sweetpea—BANG!

Georgie coughed and swiped purple soot off her cheeks. Great. Now her gift sucked and she looked like she'd caught herself on fire. Just great.

The door opened and closed, but her chimes didn't ring. Maybe that's why Georgie barely noticed that someone had come in before she registered a familiar shape emerging from the smoke.

"Nadine! What are you doing here already? I'm not ready yet—"

Nadine peered over Georgie's shoulder at the mess on her desk, her dark eyes sparkling with mischief. "Something exploded. I couldn't resist coming to see what you were up to."

A lump rose in Georgie's throat. "I... was trying to make you a gift," she said miserably. She nudged a thin black box toward Nadine. Nadine opened it and pulled out a necklace of silver links. "There's supposed to be a pendant. A tiny glass jar with a spell inside. I wanted it to hold good memories of times we were together, so that whenever you opened it, it would show you something of home."

"Wow," Nadine breathed. Her wild, dark curls haloed her face in the dim light, and Georgie felt the tears welling in her eyes again. "That's really advanced magic, Georgie."

"Yeah except it's not working." Georgie took a deep breath and squared her shoulders. "I'm sorry about... all of this. I just wanted to show you how much—" Georgie bit her lip. Glanced away. "How much you mean to me," she finished quietly.

"How much I mean to you," Nadine repeated softly, her eyes fixed on Georgie's face.

Georgie fiddled with a stalk of lavender. Flipped it over and over in her hands. Finally she looked up and said, "Give me one last try. I'll be out after that, no matter what. I promise." Nadine hesitated, and Georgie gave her a little push off the bench. "Go on. It's your party. Go enjoy it."

"I'll save you a seat," Nadine said firmly. "You'll be out soon?"

"Yes! I already promised."

"Okay then." Nadine crossed toward the door and hesitated once more. Georgie's heart gave an unwelcome twinge at the sight of her wild and wonderful best friend already in her new uniform. Gryphon Preparatory Academy for the Magically Gifted was one of the best magical boarding schools in the country; everyone knew their signature maroon and black logo of a gryphon rampant. When Georgie had pushed Nadine to apply, she'd known her best friend would get in. She'd know it would hurt when she left. But Nadine deserved this, and Georgie wasn't going to let her sadness ruin that triumph.

"I'm really proud of you, Nadine," Georgie said softly, and Nadine beamed.

"You better be. I'm going to go kick butt."

The girls giggled, and then Nadine slipped back out to the noise and bustle of the party. And Georgie knew what she needed to do.

She didn't put in any arborvitae this time. Magic didn't like when you lied, even to yourself, and the spell wouldn't work with friendship as the base.

After all, Nadine had never just been Georgie's friend.

Lavender. Because Nadine was Georgie's first crush, even though she'd never get a chance to tell her now. A yellow tulip, for the sunshine in Nadine's smile. Basil, for very good wishes. Rosemary, for remembrance. Red rose hips, for love that never bloomed. Pansy, for thoughts and a history bigger than themselves. Ivy, for friendship and fidelity.

And sweetpea. For beautiful memories. For thank you, and goodbye.

Georgie was smiling as the tears flowed down her cheeks. The mixture in front of her swirled a gorgeous teal, ribboned with cheerful yellow. Teal was Nadine's favorite color; yellow was Georgie's.

She'd done it.

"Good work," Vincent croaked, startling her. Georgie raised an eyebrow at him.

"Thanks, I guess. Fat lot of help you were, though."

"You never needed my help," Vincent replied loftily. "True magic comes from knowing yourself. Not my job to share it for you. The power's in the knowing."

Georgie latched the bauble to the chain, but hesitated before putting it back in the box. "The spell won't... tell her, will it? About how I feel?"

"Nope." Vincent settled back on his haunches. "Like I said, the power's in the knowing. No sharing necessary."

Georgie settled the necklace in its case and squared her shoulders. "Good. I'm ready to say goodbye, then." She swiped her cheeks to clean off any last tears and traces of soot, grabbed her good hat off the shelf, and opened the door, ready to find Nadine. She glanced back at her bench and paused with a small smile.

A few traces of magic drifted over the bench, and Vincent's tongue flashed out to snatch it. For a second, his body glowed silver— then he belched, and the magic was gone. For now, at least. But it was there, waiting, in the herbs and flowers scattered about the bench, in Georgie's color-splattered notebook, and in her second-best hat on its hook. And Georgie felt that spark glow within herself too—that spark of knowing who she was in this moment, even if no one else did.

And that was a little bit of magic all on its own.

T-Rex
L. W. Lewis

A tiny little T-Rex
Was scolded by his mother.
She told him it was not polite
To eat his baby brother.

The T-Rex did not know that.
Tears welled up in his eyes.
He solemnly promised Mother
To be good and not tell lies.

Which is why he will not answer
His Mother's frantic quiz.
He does not want to talk about
Where his little sister is!

Uninvited Guests
Alcuin Fromm

Emil had just finished buttoning his festive shoulder cape when Brin burst open the door to his chamber. Wide-eyed and out of breath, she paused just long enough to locate her brother before dashing across the room.

"Someone is going to be poisoned tonight," she said.

As she spoke, she grasped Emil by the arms, stretching his poor shoulder cape until the top button flew off like a bird startled out of a bush. He shook his head in confusion.

"What in Creation are you talking about?"

Brin closed her eyes and composed her youthful face, flattening her frown and relaxing her furrowed brow. After a deep breath she opened her eyes and continued.

"I just had..." Her eyes darted around and she lowered her voice. "I just had one of my visions."

Emil pursed his lips tightly and looked at his sister deeply in the eyes, trying to pierce right to her soul.

"You're certain of it?" he said.

"Yes."

His voice grew graver.

"You're absolutely certain that it was not a dream or your imagination?"

"No! I..."

Tears of frustration began to roll down Brin's flushed cheeks. Emil's stern expression vanished.

"I'm sorry," she said. "It's just—"

Emil pulled her to himself and embraced her.

"No, no, I'm the one who's sorry," he said. "I forget what a curse this is for you."

Gently pushing her back, he took her hands in his own.

"All right now," he said calmly. "What was the vision?"

She pulled away and began pacing around the chamber with an air of desperation that Emil had never seen in over sixteen years of shared life in Margu Castle.

"I saw the kitchen," she said softly. "Something there is rotten or... or... spoiled. It's poisonous. Then I saw weeping and mourning. I can't explain it, but the two images are connected in the vision. I just know that someone, or maybe many people, will die from food that is to be served at the Feast."

Emil blinked in astonishment. "The Wedding Feast?" he said.

She nodded.

"Our *brother's* Wedding Feast?"

She nodded again more quickly.

"Our brother's Wedding Feast that begins right now!?"

She nodded a third time, her sad eyes filling again with tears. It was Emil's turn to begin pacing

"Well, what can we do about it now?" he said walking back and forth, scratching his head nervously. "The guests are here, everything's prepared. We have to go out now. We're probably already late."

"I know, I know, but I'm certain of it, Emil, I'm utterly certain. The visions always feel different when they're about... death. They're much more intense. I know that some food has become deadly poisonous."

Emil stopped at the far side of the chamber and turned to look at his sister.

"Who will get poisoned?" he asked.

"I don't know."

"What food is it?"

"I don't know!"

Emil threw up his arms in exasperation.

"This is a really uncommunicative vision, Brin. Couldn't we just tell Father, I'm sure—"

She raced over to her brother.

"No, no, Emil, please, no," she said and clutched his shoulders again. "They'll send me to the Magician's Guild if anyone finds out I have... powers."

"Father would never do that," said Emil.

"That's right," agreed Brin, "*Father* would not, but he'd be powerless to stop the Guild if they found out the truth. I'd be taken away and—"

"Yes, yes, all right," said Emil, nodding. "If word got out that you see visions..." He shuddered at the thought of his sister being put in service of the mysterious Guild. "We'll just have to think of something else. But we need help. Come on, let's go!"

###

With each hurried step down the twisting corridors of Margu Castle, a bit of the happiness Emil had felt for his older brother's wedding drained from his heart. Before long, he had perfectly forgotten the beauty of the traditional ceremony earlier that afternoon and the joy and hopefulness of the day. Equally gone was his anticipation for the sumptuous Feast awaiting him and the nearly two hundred assembled family members and guests. Excitement had been replaced by panic.

Emil and Brin arrived at the chamber of Gherradie, their lifelong friend and the Squire for the Captain of the Castle Guard. Emil pounded on his door, praying that he had not already left for the Feast. After a moment, Gherradie opened the door and gave Emil a look of surprise.

"Emil, you look dreadful. What has—"

Emil grabbed Gherradie by the arm and forcefully led him back into the chamber. Brin followed close on their heels, slamming the door behind her.

"What—"

"We don't have time, Gher," said Emil. "There's an emergency."

Brin quickly recounted her story. Gherradie was the only other person in Margu Castle who was aware of Brin's powers.

"This is most inconvenient," he said, frowning and running his hand through his hair.

"That's what I thought," said Emil.

"Yes, well, I do apologize for ruining your evening, gentlemen," said Brin with bitter sarcasm. "But what do we do?"

"We should check the kitchen and see the situation there," said Gherradie. "Maybe you'll have another vision?"

She shrugged. "Anything's possible," she said, "I have no idea how these visions work. But I've never seen the same event twice."

A bell began ringing. The guests were being called to the Dining Hall. The young people stared at each other for a moment in paralyzed fear before Gherradie, always the most active of the three friends, broke their stupor.

"Follow me," he said.

He ripped open the door and vanished down the hall. Emil and Brin hurried after him.

The kitchen, normally bustling with activity, was nearly empty when they arrived. Only a handful of servants, unhappily charged with cleaning, had not already left for the Feast. Emil crossed the room and poked his head through the door to the adjacent Dining Hall. To their credit, the kitchen staff had prepared a marvelous buffet. Four long tables were simply covered with every imaginable delicacy and culinary delight, from whole fish and mountains of cured meats to pastries, tortes, and the finest desserts. And the crowning jewel of the Feast was the best pick of Margu village's enormous swine herd, slowly rotating on a spit placed on the hearth of the Dining Hall's massive fireplace.

Guests were entering from three different doors. Emil saw his father and mother, the Prince and Princess of Margu, at the head table, smiling happily and greeting people as they passed by. To their right sat the newly married couple, Emil and Brin's brother and his bride, blissfully unaware of the danger that lurked unseen before their very eyes. Emil swirled around to look at his friends in the kitchen.

"Everything's set," he said. "All the food is already out there. The guests have almost all arrived." He let out a frustrated sigh. "What if we just tell everyone? Just announce it."

"They'd never believe us," said Gherradie. "What proof could we give that didn't betray Brin's secret?"

"And besides," said Brin, "the food is still poisonous. It could be eaten later."

"Brin, are you sure you can't just tell us what is poisonous?" asked Emil desperately.

She shook her head as her lips quivered. She blinked back tears. "I wish I could."

A second bell sounded. The call to table had finished. After a few words of greeting and the prayer before meals, the food would be served. Emil stared helplessly at his sister's sorrowful face, unable to think. Suddenly, Gherradie's eyes widened. He smiled with an almost mischievous glee.

"I've got it," he said.

Emil and Brin stared at their friend in suspense. He told them his plan.

"You have got to be kidding," Emil said after Gherradie had finished.

"It's brilliant," said Brin, smiling for the first time.

Gherradie looked at each of them in turn.

"It's all we've got," he said. "Brin and I will take care of it. Emil, just do your part."

"But—"

Gherradie grabbed Brin's hand and they dashed out of the kitchen. Emil stood alone in the doorway to the Dining Hall, confronted with a nightmarish decision. He heard applause. It sounded dim, as if miles away. His head throbbed in time with his pounding heart. The Dining Hall fell silent and the Prince of Margu lowered his head to recite the prayer before meals. Emil glanced at his mother, her head likewise bowed and her eyes closed.

Suddenly, Emil imagined his parents as if they were dead, their eyes not closed in prayer, but in eternal sleep. His heart broke and terror for their lives gripped him. In a flash, he realized that nothing was more important than eliminating the danger to their lives and the lives of all the guests. He had to protect them, no matter what it took. The prince finished the prayer and raised his goblet to begin the Feast. Emil stepped out into the Dining Hall.

"Excuse me," he said in a cracking voice.

His father opened his mouth to speak.

"Excuse me!"

The Prince of Margu, together with the entire crowd of guests, turned to look at the source of the interruption, their heads moving in unison as if they had all been tied together with taut rope. He could no longer retreat from his decision. With shaking steps, Emil walked past one of the sumptuously laden tables and stepped in front of the slowly rotating pig roast at the far end of the room. The servants stared at him in shock as they kept turning the spit, its soft, rhythmic squeak becoming the only sound in the room full of wide eyes and aghast faces.

"Thank you... I... on the..."

Emil cleared his throat. Surprise was turning to annoyance among the guests, especially at the head table.

"On this... uh... special occasion, I wish to..."

Cold dread seized his heart. He didn't know what he had actually intended. He knew what Gherradie and Brin wanted him to do, but he couldn't think of how to achieve it. His mind reeled, searching for any solution. After what seemed like an eternity, a thought came to him. It leapt into his mind so suddenly that he grasped it in sheer desperation.

"I wish to honor the newly married couple with the special recitation of a song..."

He cleared his throat again as guests began to look uncomfortably from one to another, whispering and murmuring with perturbed and dismayed expressions. The prince lowered his goblet and looked at his son in pure frustration.

"The Ballad of Janth!"

Despite his panic, Emil almost laughed as he said the title. Nothing could have been more inappropriate. Gasps and audible words of consternation reached his ears. Of all the things in the world to choose, his frazzled brain decided on an eight-thousand-line tragic poem.

Emil sang.

A dreadful sight for blood-specked eyes
Through misty, downy veil
Emerged, o Muse, to claim his prize,
A warrior in mail.

With step as light as ether's sigh
Bold Janth did mount the field,
A notch for each he'd caused to die
Emblazed upon his shield.

The guests began openly to speak with each other. Emil could only imagine what they were saying as he kept singing and singing. His voice was off key. He stumbled over the words. It was a butchery of one of the greatest pieces in all Marguan literature. After fifteen or twenty stanzas, his memory began to fail him. He started making up lines, oblivious to the ballad's careful meter and rhyme scheme.

Whatever he was... intending
Had not the force of law
Because his fellow soldiers
Were... about... to betray... him

The newly married couple stared at Emil angrily. His sister-in-law tried to strangle him mentally and her fiery eyes bored holes into his skull. But Emil kept singing and singing. More than one guest had stood up and made pleading gestures to Emil's father to end the travesty. Emil's voice faltered and his throat clenched. He could barely continue.

But he never...

...because...

...and there was...

...hooooope...

The south doors flew open and slammed against the walls, making such a noise that everyone turned to look. Emil nearly collapsed in exhaustion as his voice finally faded into an inarticulate wheeze. A tense moment of silent anticipation followed.

And then the pigs came.

Like a roll of thunder, the sound of pounding hooves preceded the horrifying sight of their entrance into the Dining Hall. Dozens of squealing pigs poured into the room, falling over each other in a mad stampede. They ran between the tables, knocked over candle stands, and slammed against the benches of the terrified guests. Screams and shouts of fury filled the Hall, mixing with the shrieks of the animals to create an utter cacophony of sound.

The guests leapt to their feet and scattered in all directions like ants out of an uprooted ant hill. The doors choked with fleeing figures, pushing and shoving to get out of the room. Others pressed themselves up against the walls of the Hall to avoid contact with the muddy intruders.

It only took a moment for the pigs to discover the food. Newly emptied benches provided perfect ramps for the animals who leapt from floor to bench to table with surprising agility. Bits of smoked salmon flew in all directions. Gravy poured off the tables in cascades. Flakes of exploded pastry crust snowed to the ground.

Emil stepped onto a chair next to the fireplace and viewed the pandemonium with a mix of disgust and admiration for Gherradie's plan. The servants attending the roast had fled when a number of pigs knocked over the spit holding their deceased sibling, sending it careening backwards into the flames. The skin began to blacken and split as the smell of burning pork gave the room an appropriate odor to match the visual spectacle.

The prince shouted commands in an attempt to maintain order. When he saw Gherradie and Brin standing in the doorway, he called over to them.

"Brin, dear, are you all right? Try to pass the word among the guests to meet at the Kinnik Tavern in the village. We'll have a reception there."

"Yes, Father!" she yelled back and disappeared.

"Squire?"

"Your highness?" said Gherradie

"Help the Castle Guard and get these beasts out of here!"

"Yes, your highness."

Most of the guests had fled, with only a few oglers remaining, and the pigs had settled themselves into a relatively calm grazing. The prince slid along the wall, staying clear of the animals, and came over to his son.

"What a disaster. How in Creation could this have happened?"

Emil said nothing, mesmerized by the sight of a particularly enthusiastic pig gnawing liver pâté off a wooden serving platter.

"And why did you start reciting poetry, Son? Badly, I might add. You couldn't have chosen a worse time."

Emil cleared his throat.

"On the contrary, I felt that the situation required it, Father."

"What a disaster," he said again distractedly.

"I'll stay here and help with these pigs," said Emil.

"Yes, good, thank you," said his father as he made his way to the door. "What a disaster. And then get yourself over to the Tavern. We'll have a Feast for your brother yet or I'm not the Prince of Margu."

###

Brin walked into the Dining Hall. Gherradie and a handful of the Castle Guard were rounding up the last of the pigs, and Emil sat on the ground, carefully scraping

74

whipped cream off an ancient tapestry. She walked over to Emil and gave him a lopsided smile.

"Well, we did it," she said. "For better or for worse."

Emil nodded.

"How did you keep them from starting the Feast?" she asked.

Emil told her about his spontaneous inspiration to become a bard. She laughed.

"I'm sorry I missed it. You can try again at the Tavern."

"No, thank you," he said. "One time was already too much."

Gherradie came over to them. Emil reached out a hand and Gherradie grasped it, helping Emil stand up.

"We're almost finished here," said Gherradie. "Just a few more to go." He grinned and lowered his voice so that only they could hear. "It was easier to get them to stampede than to round them all back up. I don't envy the poor souls who'll have to clean up this mess."

"But it was necessary," said Brin. "I know it."

"I sure hope so," said Emil. "The consequences from this whole thing are—"

A piercing shriek cut him off. They all turned to look in the direction of the sound. There was another shriek, then a low bellowing. One of the pigs stumbled out from behind an overturned chair. It tottered forward a few steps, made a gagging sound, then collapsed. The three friends exchanged knowing glances.

"Lieutenant," said Gherradie to one of the Guard. "Tell the Captain to make sure that pig is buried and not butchered for food. It is clearly sick and should not be eaten."

"Good idea, Squire."

Two of the Guard hoisted up the animal and carried it out of the Dining Hall, leaving the three standing alone. Gherradie turned to Brin.

"No liquids are poisonous, right Brin? Just food?"

"Yes," she said.

Gherradie found a bottle of cider in the deserted kitchen. Then the three friends sat in the empty Dining Hall and toasted the ruins of their success.

Toad

Vonnie Winslow Crist

Forward Control Thrusters

Katarzyna Lisińska

You were supposed to scrutinise some
binary-like oxidative-something cells.
In space.

Always yearning for attention,
you weren't an exception.
I don't have a grudge against you.
You sent the video about your mission.
Quite interesting.

I can only remember flight deck, star
trackers and forward control thrusters.

Everyone has his own definition of a hero.
There is said we must learn the tolerance.

Now, I can only dab the smooth surface of a
picture, recalling warm touch of your fingers
in my palm.

I am standing on the landing platform,
glaring upon the sky.
I catch a glimpse of a shooting star,
pondering about my deplorably wishful
thinking.

The universe won't be real for me,
as long as you're not there.

A Boy and His Dragonfly

Colin had to leave his dog behind when his family left Earth. Now they're on Verte. He's new, and has no friends. His older sister gets her choice of everything. He gets the smallest bedroom . . . but he gets first choice of companions!

Type: Short story – digital – science fiction

Audience: children and young adults

Ordering Link:

ePub ($1.29):
https://www.hiraethsffh.com/product-page/copy-of-boy-and-his-dragonfly-by-tyree-campbell

pdf ($1.29):
https://www.hiraethsffh.com/product-page/boy-and-his-dragonfly-by-tyree-campbell

The Caves of Titan
By Debby Feo

Students at the Galileo Interplanetary School explore new-found caves on Titan, where they encounter the Cenote People and learn to get along with them—and with each other, as they continue to grow and learn in a diverse student body. Still, there are conflicts to resolve . . . and some of them might put an end to the school!

Ordering link:

Print Edition ($10.00):
https://www.hiraethsffh.com/product-page/caves-of-titan-by-debby-feo

Scriptolographic Wizards

Alan J Wahnefried

"You can't make me become a wizard!" Melanie pouted.

"You are right," Master Gustavus replied calmly.

"I never wanted to be a wizard!" Melanie charged.

"I am sure you never considered the possibility," the master responded.

"Why did you think I would want to be a wizard?" Melanie ranted on.

"Before I answer your last question, I need you to answer a question of mine," Gustavus said. "What is a wizard?"

"What's a wizard? Wizards are those weird people you see in books with long gowns covered in symbols. They turn people into toads," Melanie retorted.

Master Gustavus chuckled before replying. "If someone is called a pinball wizard, do they turn the person at the next machine into a gerbil when they don't get a free game?"

"Well, no," Melanie replied in an uncertain voice.

"If someone is a tech wizard, do they wear a weird gown?" Gustavus probed.

"Don't get me started about prom. Some techies do dress funny. I don't think I've seen any in gowns, even at prom. Why are you asking me these things?" Melanie shot back.

I guess I hit a sore spot, Gustavus thought. *I am not going to ask about her prom.*

"Both of us need to be talking about the same thing," Master Gustavus began. "The term wizard has multiple meanings. Most people's minds go to where you came from. We need to use the same context."

Melanie composed herself. "What context are you using? Culinary wizard?"

Gustavus laughed. "Heavens, no. People get called wizards when they can inexpiably and easily do things others can't. Scriptolographic Guild members get called wizards as we can read and write cursive scripts. Most people see cursive and hieroglyphics as essentially the same."

"We think you may have requisite abilities to be a wizard but lack training," he continued. "We want to talk about both. You may have the capabilities to join our Guild."

"What? Why do you think I have those capabilities?" a puzzled Melanie asked.

Gustavus paused for a moment. "I know you got caught flat-footed by this interview. The answer to your question is simple. Can I offer you some water, or a snack, before I explain?" he said.

What type of weird thing is this? Melanie asked herself.

"A bottle of water would be nice," she replied, stalling.

Gustavus retrieved two bottles of water from a small refrigerator. He handed one to Melanie.

"Please answer my questions. What I am going to say will not make much sense on first hearing," he began.

Melanie nodded.

"Do you remember going to science museums, or children's museums, when you were in grade school?", he asked.

"Well, yes. My class went at least once a semester," she replied.

"Did the museum give every person a special name tag with their name on it? I presume someone scanned the nametags," he continued.

"I guess so. It wasn't a big deal," Melanie replied.

"Those tags are why we think you have special abilities," Gustavus said.

"Wearing a nametag proves nothing. Are the rest of the class somewhere around here?" she demanded.

"You're the only one the Guild selected from your classes. You weren't selected because you looked cute with a name tag. Your behavior over time caused us to pay attention to you. We weren't attracted to you by any one thing. Please be patient," he said,

I might as well see this thing through, Melanie thought. She nodded again.

"When your class went to the museum, did they start seeing an exhibit, like dinosaurs or airplanes?" Gustavus probed.

"Yes. That's why we went," Melanie conceded.

"After the exhibits, you had an activity session. The activity area had several things to do. Some activities were simple, like making a paper airplane. Other activities involved making something more complicated with adults to help you. Right?" the wizard asked.

"Most of the kids were elbowing each other at the easy stuff. I thought the other stuff was more interesting. Why are you asking?" Melanie replied.

"The Scriptolographic Guild doesn't monitor every museum. We did monitor the museums around your home," he began. "We captured a list of children in the more challenging activities."

"You are not making sense," she said.

"I am describing a pattern. Did the pattern hold through most of your grade school?" he said.

Melanie had to think. *Who remembers grade school field trips?* She thought about it, and a pattern emerged.

"Now that you mention it, yes," she answered.

"As you got older, the challenging stuff got more difficult. You kept trying the complicated tasks. Where did you assemble your first jigsaw puzzle?" Gustavus continued.

"In a museum," she recalled.

"Do you still enjoy them?" he asked.

"Yes, I do."

"What about three-dimensional puzzles? Do you like them?" Gustavus asked.

"Yes. I tried the first one on a field trip," Melanie replied uncertainly.

Gustavus handed Melanie a pad of paper and a pencil. "Would you please write your name for me?" he asked.

Melanie printed her name with a shrug.

"Can your classmates do what you just did?" Gustavus probed.

"I doubt it," she replied.

"Where did you learn? In school?" he asked.

"Not in school. I attended a summer art class when I was in middle school. That's where I learned to write with a pencil," she replied. "You're going to take credit for that class?"

"Yes, I am," the wizard said. "We kept winnowing down our sample. The Guild offered the class to you and several of your classmates. You were the only one from your school who attended. Do you ever write stuff on paper?"

"Most stuff I write, like class notes, I just type on my computer," she began. "Personal stuff, like a poem, I usually start on paper. It feels better."

"Very good. Do you keep a diary?"

"How did you know?" she demanded.

Are these guys mind readers? She asked herself.

"I guessed," he explained. "Most of our members keep a diary or journal."

"Do you play your violin in the acoustic mode often?" Gustavus probed.

"How do you know about my violin? Is this some dark government agency?" Melanie blurted out in exasperation.

"We are not part of any government. Our Guild Hall is on Grand Cayman, the Switzerland of the Western Hemisphere. We know about the violin from your high school orchestra's concert programs. When we identify a possible member, we keep scanning the internet. Would you answer my question, please?"

"Sorry about the outburst," Melanie replied. "I use the acoustic mode for my own enjoyment. The electronic mode is like lip-synching. We can't use acoustic mode in class or at concerts."

"Can you sight-read music?" the master asked.

"I have tried," she replied. "The result wasn't great."

"Have you ever tried playing a piece of music you've heard but don't have the music," he asked.

"If the music was interesting and I'm bored, I have tried. I get pretty close to the original," she said proudly.

Gustavus handed Melanie a sheet of paper with a paragraph written in cursive.

"Can you read that?" he asked.

Melanie hesitated. "Some of it, maybe. Other parts look weird," she replied.

"I didn't think you would be able to. I had to ask. I know enough to give a full explanation. Do you need a break?" Gustavus said.

"I'm good," she replied.

"Would you like to move to a more comfortable chair?" he asked.

"Why not?" she replied.

This wooden chair is better for interrogation than conversation, she thought.

The pair moved away from Gustavus' desk to a conversation area.

The pair settled into upholstered chairs surrounding a coffee table. Gustavus gestured to an open box of candy in the table's center.

"The candies are chocolate-covered cherries and chocolate-covered marshmallows. Please help yourself," he offered.

How did they know my favorite chocolates? she wondered.

"Thanks," she replied, selecting a piece.

"Where to begin?" Gustavus began. "A long time ago, people learned their letters and numbers on paper with pencils?"

"Now everything is digitized. We learn on tablets and keyboards," Melanie rejoined.

"Not everything is digitized," he responded. "Everything that seemed important at the time was digitized. Many things that seemed unimportant, or were unknown, weren't digitized."

"Like what?" Melanie asked, intrigued.

"Universities receive collections of papers from alumni or estates. Most universities have large collections of unindexed papers written in cursive," Gustavus answered. "People have old journals and papers."

"The piece of cursive I showed you is from the diary of Mary Drumthawicit," he continued. "She lived during the American Civil War. There was a small battle in Arkansas. One of the generals made questionable actions. His actions are still debatable. Mrs. Drumthawicit's diary described troops passing her farm. Her information exonerated the general. The diary surfaced in the last five years. Most people can't read the diary. That's where Scriptolographic wizards come in."

"You just type old documents into a computer?" she asked.

"It's more than typing. We interpret archaic expressions and usage. Our process is more like translation than transcription," Gustavus said. "In the case of the diary, the digital version of the journal became the basis of a Ph.D. thesis. The dissertation contained images of pages from the diary. The translating wizard certified the images' accuracy. The wizard got partial credit for the dissertation."

Reading musty dusty documents does not sound interesting, Melanie thought.

"We don't go look for the documents. The documents are cleaned and conserved before we start work," he concluded.

Where is he getting his information? Melanie fumed, trying to keep a poker face.

"Is that all?" she asked.

"Are you up for adventures?" Gustavus asked.

"Like what?" Melanie asked.

"There are still unexplored parts of the world," the wizard began. "We all think of these expeditions using digital gear. The capabilities of digital gear are limited. Batteries go dead. Satellites are unavailable. Tablets get destroyed. The most robust recording device is a tablet of paper in a waterproof pouch. Recording information on paper requires a guild member."

"I'd be there just to take notes?" she asked.

"Our people synthesize, analyze, and record the expedition's work," Gustavus said. "The analysis is a key part of their role and value to the expedition."

He paused to take a candy from the box.

"You mentioned you like to write on paper. Do you ever draw on it?" Gustavus asked.

"Why are you changing the subject? Yes, I do sketch occasionally. I'm not very good," she replied.

"I understand your accusation. I am not changing the topic. Some primitive people have never seen an electronic tablet. They'd think their soul had been stolen if they saw a full-color image of themselves. What happens next is not pretty," he explained.

"Such expeditions carry a wizard who can sketch and transcribe," he said. "The sketches are a crucial part of the expedition's records."

"I asked about your music as expeditions may need to record their subject's music. Electronic copies of music have the same problem as electronic images. A wizard being able to write down music they've heard is invaluable," Gustavus continued. "Also, every language and document has its own rhythm. A music background helps pick up the rhythm."

Expeditions could be alluring, she thought.

"Any other possibilities?" she asked.

"What else is still only written in cursive?" he retorted. "Some wizards translate heirloom recipes at community events. You'd be surprised how many legal documents, like deeds, birth certificates, and wills, only exist in cursive. Genealogy records contain cursive. Some wizards are experts in experts in languages like Latin, German, or Swedish. Others are cryptographers. Your imagination and market sense are the only limits."

"What's your specialty?" Melanie asked, trying to turn the tables.

"Medieval music," the master replied proudly. "I must know music, Latin, and several other languages. The amount of material needing interpretation defies belief."

"What does your wife think you do?" she continued.

"She knows I am a tenured professor at the College of King Haakon V," Gustavus replied. "I will be catching a flight back to campus later today."

Touché, Gustavus thought. *She does have potential.*

A coy smile played over Melanie's face. "What next?" she asked.

"You have to make a decision," Gustavus replied. "You can tell me one of three things. You can say no, yes, or ask for more time. I must warn you. You can't change your mind."

"If I say no. What happens? Do you turn me into a gerbil?" she gently taunted.

"We don't turn people into gerbils," Gustavus said with a smile. "I will thank you for your time. My assistant will cover your expenses. You will never hear from us again."

"And if I say yes?" she inquired.

"Saying yes is like signing up for a trade school," he began. "We will talk about courses at another interview. Saying yes isn't a guarantee you will become a wizard. We will start your training."

"What about the third option?" she needed to know.

"You do not get an infinite amount of time. You are probably thinking about your future profession," he replied. "We want you to begin training as a wizard as soon as we can. You will get emails asking for a decision or describing courses. At some point, we will demand a decision," he finished.

"I am thinking about going to college. How would that fit in?" Melanie asked.

"College and wizardly are not mutually exclusive," Gustavus replied. "If you choose to go to college first, we will give you more time for your decision. If you become a wizard first, the guild may pay for your college."

"I should add we do not cloister our candidates. We want you to have a normal life with our unusual profession," he concluded.

"I am intrigued," Melanie said, trying to sound reserved. "This is too much to process. I will take your third option. What next?"

"Most possible candidates take the third option. I record your choice is the obvious answer," Gustavus replied. He extracted a large envelope from his desk and handed it to Melanie.

"Open it," he began. "This is our gift to you."

Melanie opened the envelope. She extracted multiple pamphlets, a package of ballpoint pens, pieces of paper with blank music staffs, and a notebook with her name and the Scriptolographic Guild's logo embossed on the cover.

"What is this stuff?" a bewildered Melanie asked.

"The pamphlets describe courses on cursive script, transcribing and writing music, and sketching with pencils," the wizard replied. "The pamphlets contain vouchers to pay for the courses. The music paper allows you to experiment with writing your chords. The notebook would make a great diary. A diary written in cursive is automatically encrypted. You write with pencils. I am giving you pens, so you can try writing with them. Let me show you how to use the pens."

Gustavus retrieved a scrap of paper. He showed Melanie how to use a pen. Melanie tried and was pleasantly surprised.

"Weren't you gambling embossing my name on the notebook?" she asked.

Having my name embossed is scary, she thought. *How much do these guys know?*

"We didn't gamble much," he replied. "We can pop the paper out of the cover. The cover is only vinyl. We didn't know if you would accept or not. You are a special person. We wanted to show you that we want you to join us. Take the remaining candies if you want. My wife says I eat too many. You've seen the candies don't turn people into gerbils."

Melanie laughed, shook Gustavus's hand, and left with her gifts.

###

Melanie discussed the Scriptolographic Guild with her parents. Her parents were supportive after they asked numerous questions. They thought their daughter was magical, but a wizard was on a different level.

"It would be nice if you learned cursive," Melanie's mother said.

"Why?" Melanie asked.

"I have my great-grandma's diary. I can't read it," her mom replied. "I'd like to know what she has to say."

Melanie had never heard of the diary.

###

Later she started looking at the brochures.

The cursive course might let me read the diary, she thought. *The course could be a good way to check. out this wizard stuff. I like the idea of encrypting my diary.*

The adventure began.

Who?

Ann Hoekstra is an artist located in Minnesota. She works with digital media and ink sketches. Her pandemic hobby has been making oil paintings of dogs in old Victorian poses.

Vonnie Winslow Crist is an award-winning author/illustrator. Her fantastical stories, poems, and art are published in Australia, Japan, India, Italy, Spain, Germany, Finland, Canada, the UK and USA. For more info: http://www.vonniewinslowcrist.com

James Fitzsimmons writes sf, fantasy, and horror. James loves writing for youth, when the senses of wonder and adventure are at their peak! Links to James's fiction can be found on his LinkedIn page at https://www.linkedin.com/in/james-

<u>fitzsimmons-064ba150</u> "Luke & Odett" was first published in the anthology, *Rockets and Robots*.

Megan Archibeque is a writer of fiction, and especially loves her sci-fi and fantasy. She graduated with a BFA in creative writing from Boise State University. She has been previously published in The Disappointed Housewife and Mister Magazine.

Grant Swenson is an aerospace engineer, working in the satellite industry, who loves writing fantasy and science-fiction for all ages. Over the last decade, his plays have been featured by various theater groups in Colorado. He is an active member of SCBWI.

Megan Mahoney is a middle school teacher with an English Literature and Creative Writing degree and a Masters in Classical Education from Eastern University. The first chapter of her Young Adult fantasy manuscript has been published in the journal *Workings Classicists*; her other publications include *Ethel Zine* magazine, and Eastern's *Inklings* journal, which she later edited. She has also received the Benjamin Carr award for journalism. In her spare time, she enjoys cooking and baking, making color-coded research plans for future vacations, and hanging out with her younger siblings.

Mr. Wahnefried lives in a suburb of Detroit, Michigan, with his charming and understanding wife. He graduated from the University of Michigan. After a career in IT, he is either an experienced programmer or an old hacker.

Alcuin Fromm is an American living in Germany. A lifelong lover of fantasy and science fiction, his literary dream is to craft stories that transport his readers to far-away worlds where they might find a souvenir to bring back home to the real one.

Lisa Timpf's speculative poetry has appeared in a variety of magazines and anthologies. When not writing, Lisa enjoys organic gardening, bird-watching, and walking her lively Jack Russel-cocker spaniel Chet. You can find out more about Lisa's writing at http://lisatimpf.blogspot.com/.

L. W. Lewis is a retired U.S. Air Force pilot and navigator. He was assigned to B-52's during the Viet Nam War and later flew fighters with the Flying Tigers. While assigned as an advisor to the US Army he completed jump school and has made 268 military parachute jumps. He holds a BS degree from the University of Miami in Florida and an MS degree from Oklahoma City University. His introduction to poetry began in the sixth grade and has been a part of his life ever since.

Lauren McBride finds inspiration in faith, family, nature, science, and membership in the SFPA. Nominated for the Best of the Net, Pushcart, Rhysling, and Dwarf Stars Awards, her poetry has appeared internationally in speculative and mainstream publications including *Asimov's, Fantasy & Science Fiction,* and *Utopia Science Fiction's 5th Anniversary Anthology.* Her chapbook, *Aliens, Magic, and Monsters,* was published by Hiraeth (2023). She enjoys swimming, gardening, baking, reading, writing, and knitting scarves for U.S. troops.

Lisa Lahey has been an elementary school teacher for 27 years. She has one grown daughter named Jessica. She has been published in 34th Parallel Magazine.

Kate Lisińska is Polish and is passionate about science fiction and study of culture . She is also interested in astronomy and geography. She was living and working in Finland and the UK , currently based in Germany. In her free time she likes skiing, writing and travelling.

Brian Rosenberger lives in a cellar in Marietta, GA and writes by the light of captured fireflies. He is the author of As the

Worm Turns and three poetry collections - Poems That Go Splat, And For My Next Trick..., and Scream for Me.

www.ingramcontent.com/pod-product-compliance
Lightning Source LLC
Chambersburg PA
CBHW052114150726
48002CB00006B/2342